I0424568

The Poetic Musings of a Rambling Mind

Author
Micki Hogan

©2019

ISBN 9781076708908
independently published

About the Author
Micki Hogan is a published author

The Poetic Musings of a Rambling Mind

who writes
on a variety of subjects.

Her poetry has be called an
inspirational
stepping stone for others.
Her short fiction has allowed her
to once be called
the V.C. Andrews of our time.
Her children lullaby books
have been sold internationally
and she is currently working on
Volume III
of her Fairy's Lullaby Collection.

She is a long time advocate
for Service Dogs,
the disease Ankylosing Spondylitis
and the Civil Rights of
Disabled Individuals

Dedication
This book is dedicated to those who fear

3

Micki Hogan
©2019

being lost within their mind.
Writing has become a healing tool for me
and I hope that these ramblings
are enjoyed by many.
Although the words may make no sense
they are the words that
allowed me to find my center
when I was lost and confused.

I wish to thank my husband
for being there
when I needed him most.
This is something I will never forget.
He is my hero.
He is my soulmate.
I love you, my lover

To my twins,
Donnie Ray and Danny Ray
Forever my Narkals
I love You

Time to make a magic wish
Behold the unfinished obelisk
Where true secrets are held
Next cross the 45th parallel
Keep the sun on your back
Never looking back
Turn true north, set sail
Starlit nights never fail
Lunar rotation makes it mark
Summoning heavens spark

Welcome to the maze
You may become lost for days
Follow the Mystic Shrines
Riding on Golden clouds that shine
A vow of silence welcomes the truth
Scream loudly now,
never be subdued
Generations passed down
the knowledge
Thirteen hidden
behind cryptic markings

Micki Hogan
©2019

Blessed is those
who are graced
within the light
Bountiful delight
The harmonic glows so bright
Each waking hour it calls to all
Oh what a sight
Reaching out
to those captive by fright
Hands extended
invoking the human right
Love peace and harmony
Each incredible insight
Even in the darkest of nights
Hold tight...
Embrace the Light
Sent from a messenger
who LOVES the Light.
For it has many names

There is thirteen

Micki Hogan
©2019

who sit at the tables round
Only one who wears the crown
Others, guardians of the light
Protecting her with all their might
There is leaders and there are sheep
But it is the warriors
who protect the crown
and the meek
Knights who stand tall
not afraid to lose it all
These are who we choose to be
Protectors of those who see
And those who could never be
There is a pendulum
that sways both ways
Both during the night and day
To embrace the future if you can
Always protecting the secrets
passed down
Either in a heart or in a sacred chest
Always protect the codex
Mystic shrines
can read between the lines
Always Embrace the light
Hold it tight
Even in the darkest of nights
Eyes wide open

Behold her opulent heart
Lavished right from the start
A princess with nothing of need
Truth of the world she did not see
Until she stepped outside her box
She no longer looked down
from the top
She found a world
that needed her love
She was graced with love from
above

9

Micki Hogan
©2019

There is a tale as old as time
Passed down in rhythmic rhyme
From the old ways to a seer's demure
Pyramids topped with copper
Reveal a recycled future
Sitting at the table round
Secrets hidden deep underground
Names kept withheld
Changed in ever book or tale

Micki Hogan
©2019

Although the trail is twisted
I have a journey in which I am enlisted
To embrace the glory of this world
To make sure the silent is heard
So many alone and scared
Feeling as though no one cares
I care for you my friends
Together we fight this battle
until the end

Micki Hogan
©2019

Energy invokes the power inside
Plethora of reasons divide
Cannon of thoughts elude
This vortex cannot be subdued
Waking hours before Dawn
Thunder roars it's powerful song
Elements of Grandeur persists
Purgatory's conundrum
never to be dismissed

12

Micki Hogan
©2019

When the Roseline crosses
the 45th parallel
Follow the magpies
that you see
Do not enter No Mans Land
Pass the Vail
Just beyond No Name
Head Due North
To where ashes are meant
to be spread
Hold Your Cards
Never to speak the words
For this is the code of X

Micki Hogan
©2019

They said our fairy tale can't be true
What was a princess to do
She calls out to the land
Welcoming harmony
with both hands
Only those enchanted know
the nightingales song
She had still remembered
after so long

14

The Earth trembles with delight
Making way to Tranquility Bay
Open arms giving back in hindsight
Captivated by the messages
received today
A path to enlightened life
Is simply a lifetime away

15

Micki Hogan
©2019

Catch a rainbow
in crystal prisms
Wear copper to
embrace the magnetism
Keep the secrets
of your medicine bag sacred
Always give back the energy
that you borrow
Let natures song
cure your sorrow
Fear not the light you seek
Be grateful you are able
to take a peek

Micki Hogan
©2019

Nightly
Star Gazing
Catching Glimpse
Single Gentle Firefly
Illuminating Night Sky
A Satellite Passes by
Catching Glimpse
Star Gazing
Nightly

17

Micki Hogan
©2019

Entangled thoughts
Do not let me be
I do not like to feel this alive
Stop, Dance, Boogey
Do another hand jive
Epic mania
Two sides meet
Epic Confrontation

Micki Hogan
©2019

Four were chosen
One was selected
Do not doubt those who get tested
He could shoot five arrows at once
Where was he buried
Never to be known
is my hunch
The code of X
Beyond the walls
Ones who always stood tall
The owl holds the clu

Magic caught in time
A plethora of dreams
Divine
Breaking through
old boundaries
Stepping forth
into destiny
Into the future
so surreal

20

Sweet Reverie
Tender Serenity
Welcoming Tranquility
Embracing Harmony
Enter Epiphany
Accepting Light
Gracefully

21

Travel to the Eye of Africa
Fear not the daughters of Denial
False Prophets steer you wrong
Beware of the unspoken song
You do not know
the meaning of it's truth
Taught to sing from a tender youth
Blessed are children of the stars
The color indigo is what they are

Micki Hogan
©2019

Copper roofs
Hold the truth
Hidden deep underneath
The City of light
Tales of such grief
Pyramids deep in Forest green
Will the last book be seen?
Lost above in sacred lies
Is the secrets they try to hide
Twisted lines crack a smile
We search blindly all the while

23

Micki Hogan
©2019

Reflecting, I look to dawn
and ask myself
Where has my confidence gone

I know I am meant to remember
Although my heart
feels utter somber
If you don't learn
from the hand of fate
How to know the path to take

Micki Hogan
©2019

Broken is minds that do not see
All the things that could be
Coded into an eternal soul
Messages they do not know
From Letters A to X
Holding Cards is always Best
Do not fear to Be Moved
Truly noble have nothing to prove
Look into your soul
Growth is the goal

13 stand tall
23 to see truth
Follow the numbers
Questions to be unraveled
A maze underneath the strata
How deep does the rabbit hole go
A plethora of knowledge below
Look to above to absorb data
23 to see the truth
13 stand tall

26

Sun rises to meet dew kissed grass
Morning glory petals embrace
Baby doves sing their songs of love
As butterflies waken
to enlightened truth
Precious is the world's youth

27

Micki Hogan
©2019

Deep into the looking glass I stare
I see you sitting right there
How dare you laugh at me
Your insanity cannot be
Taunted by words that hurt
Judged by a harsh cold world
I know your kryptonite
The powerful venom inside
Veins carry poison you seek
Run away and weep

Micki Hogan
©2019

The Serpents slither
Coaxing, Waiting. Lurking
Boundaries they can not pass
Coiled tightly,
Slanted eyes keep searching

29

I looked to West
Through my windows
I see the Beartooths at rest
Ominous, looming over all things
Majestic, yet Silent
Young eyes take in the Sight
to be seen
The Grandeur hides the Pass
To Volcanic treasures
Enduring times Faithful test

Micki Hogan
©2019

The awakened heart
cannot be denied
Look beyond
the plethora of lies
Some will tell twisted tales
While light waits
to set things right
Beware false prophets
soon they will forget
Even they were heaven sent
Fear not a thing called love
It rains down from above

Ombre clouds kiss the rising sun
Iridescent sunbeams break forth
Invoking a morning bird's song
Tender is the love that exudes

32

Micki Hogan
©2019

Music of the world sets the beat
Sounds of harmony defeat
Capture the song of pure nature
Protecting beauty for the future
Follow the winds of change
Making sure nothing is in vain
Deep into the catacombs
Secrets hidden deep
Safe from those who roam

33

Micki Hogan
©2019

There once was a seer
The outside world they feared
There once was a muse
Their words carefully choosed
There once was a warrior
Battling fate, an evil destroyer
There once was a foe
Longing for control
There once was a king
The creator of all things

34

Micki Hogan
©2019

Cryptic Letters from Past
Hidden words from Seven Eleven
Secrets cannot Last
Read between lines again
Three Times Zones in one
Patterns seen only from Strata
Follow path to forgotten Home
Beware of blinded
They see not one iota
How long will the Wanderers roam?

Micki Hogan
©2019

Opulent Demeanor
Ambient Love
Ethereal Droplets
Illuminate Passion
Tied Gossamer
Connecting Incandesce
A Plethora of Enchantment
Utterly Captivating
Gossamer wings
Requiem of waking dreams

Monks sit quietly
Meditating
Monastery atop
Mountains of Jade
Copper Roofs
always hesitating
Data hidden in
Strata,
long delayed
Stonehenge communicating
Gypsy Roma called forth
on this day
Whom sat in Shadows
waiting
Stepping into Light
Messengers no more
Depraved

37

Micki Hogan
©2019

**Do not doubt the heart
of an idle mind
Life lived in vain, so sublime
Invoke harmony
Never turning from destiny
Love, laugh, and let live
Never be afraid to forgive**

38

Ancient texts made of gold
Messages past down from
time of old
Merlin never spoke his name
King Arthur did the same
Robin Hood, a beggar in disguise
His name protected until demise
Jehovah was not his name either
Twisted scriptures to fool believers

Micki Hogan
©2019

I have been considering
a play on words
Perhaps a Ballad or a Sonnet
Would a Quatrain be so absurd
Oh, to drop ink so nonchalant

Micki Hogan
©2019

Sacred Secrets Kept
Forbidden Ground
where Moses stepped
Lonely Mountain from Tibet
Upon the hill of Avalon
The Blood of the Son Long Gone
Portals lead to Hidden Realms
Parallel Continuums
Noctilucent Paths Unseen
Only lit by Full Moon Beams

41

Micki Hogan
©2019

An epiphany most welcomed
A blessing comes in disguise
Enchanting moments become
Harmony invokes only if you try

Micki Hogan
©2019

Beauty surrounds
Harmonic sounds
Birds morning song
Squirrels scampering on ground
White cotton clouds
floating along
Graceful is a morning's dawn

43

Micki Hogan
©2019

2+2=4
Watching you once more
1+1=2
Nothing left to do
13+2=15
Man created Element 115
1+1+1=3
Patterns of Destiny
5+5=10
Rejuvenation begins
14-1=13
You already know if you believe
4+3=7
Only one path to Heaven

44

Nostradumas
Visionary Quatrains
A Mighty Earthquake
Shook every Californian
Beware Volcano Rumbles
Welcome Global Translations
Heat Waves in Ice come to pass
Animals speak if you Listen
Aged look so Young
The Womb not Sacred
War of Money begun

When darkness falls upon thy heart
Come forth, where a journey starts
Just beyond the trembles
A ring of fire awakens, it signals
A message from Mother Earth
Invoke the Light that shines down
Sheep fear not the Lion's crown
Welcome the ascended ones

Micki Hogan
©2019

Etched in stone leads a trail
Every heart of light unveiled
Follow the compass back in time
Mystic Shrines read between lines
Sacred stones guard harmonic sounds
That seep up from the ground
Always sleep with your head
pointed north
Secrets passed down from before

47

Micki Hogan
©2019

Hidden faces of 13
Element 115
Planet 4 unseen
White haired angels intervene
Mirrored writing sets the scene
Golden scrolls hidden forest green
Planet X so pristine
Element 115
Hidden faces of 13

Micki Hogan
©2019

It came within a dream
Mystic shrines
Read between the lines
They passed down a story so old
Never knowing the unwritten code
The seer has said the word
And past along the message
never to be heard
Embrace the light
The Lion sleeps tonight
It has been eons
Welcome Zion

49

Micki Hogan
©2019

Transcendence calls me
Passion of life overwhelming
Embracing heavens delight
Harmonic balance in sight
Taking in the reverie
An awakening ephinany
Looking at life's greater hand
Teaching love can save this land

50

For centuries they have searched
For the one who has no name
For she never knew it
That is until now
The secret passed down somehow
Legend speaks of a gifted child
Born in the edge of the wild
The name she keeps in her head
Part of a secret never to be said

I feel within the grace from God
The giver of Light from above
I feel with each step Mother Earth
I feel pain we have caused her
Together they bring unity to us
Uniting creating life
For them I trust
I hear the future of technology
Calling me with such longing

52

Micki Hogan
©2019

North by North East
Sitting on tilted Axis
Does the Moral Compass
Still point true North
Silent trains rumble on
Until quarter half past dawn
Playing with FM dials
Tread lightly now
Daughters of denial
Twisted words so it seems
Never to speak
3 unknown things

Micki Hogan
©2019

Secrets never to be told
Testing messengers record
Light sent them here
The unknown seers
Names unknown to the world
Isn't that absurd
Connected in unimaginable ways
Only a few know games they play
Tested by those who watch
Who is strong enough to stop the clock

Micki Hogan
©2019

Slipping into the rabbit hole
A place only I know
No one can find me there
I prefer to sit in solace
Than deal with
the Jabberwocky taunting us

55

Micki Hogan
©2019

Three days in one
A perpetual pendulum
Just beyond the Prime Meridian
Carefully look now
Step so lightly where you speak
Ancient texts will need deciphered
Looking over shoulder
Behold the courage of the meek
Time eluded by everyone
Pain of a world undone
Three days in one

56

A poetic muse before I leave
A moment of solidarity what I need
My emotions have run amuck
Pondering thoughts become stuck
Learning to adjust constant battle
My nerves tethered yet unraveled
Always such a brave demure
Always paranoid of things I fear

Micki Hogan
©2019

Behold the pursuit of knowledge
The wake of humble homage
Each generation passes down
Secrets of truth so profound
Enlightenment of the blessed
Passion of life is the test
To seek a future of compassion
This is the final lesson
Seek the light
Embrace it tight

Micki Hogan
©2019

My pen will always flow
Despite what you think
The words inside always grow
Muse has thoughts so distinct
As fingers dance cross keyboard
My words become defenders
ready at the sword
Many sentences I will drop
I carry on, published or not
Doubt not the words I say

Micki Hogan
©2019

Sun sets as mustangs play
Jaguars soak in sun
Shadows grow long
End of day
Twilight shimmers
As the world re-centers

Micki Hogan

Ethereal Reflections
Tied Gossamer
Extracting Effervescence
Plethora of Serendipity
Eloquent Tranquility
Pristine Axiom
Quintessential Paradox
A Requiem of Things Unseen
Opulent Demeanor
Ambient Love

Blessed is the soul that grows
Seeking what others long to know
Reaching out for harmony
The light welcomes all who see
Feel the energy that surrounds
Deep within it can be found
Fear not the truth
It calls to you

Micki Hogan
©2019

There is a song inside my head
I know the truth of it
Once it has been said
So I will not sing this lullaby
For I fear the mourning will cry
For today is not that day
Live long my fair Lady

Micki Hogan
©2019

Mystic Shrines
Read between the lines
Behold daughters of Denial
Twisted words crack a smile
Always to be Looking overhead
Never to be looking back they said
How can the future meet the past
Eternity's infinite Looking Glass

Micki Hogan
©2019

Listen to the beat
Harmony you seek
Learn to Soar
Holding back no more
Feel the elements surround
Beyond four in this ground
Look to the air
Embracing fate with care
Behind the enlightened eye
Is where the awakened thrive
Stars already aligned
Truth no longer denied

65

Micki Hogan
©2019

Can't go back now
We've made contact
Baby if I could turn back time
I would do more than rhyme
Tell you a secret or two
We never had anything to prove
Portals within realms
Broken wings prepared to sail

Micki Hogan
©2019

We always known your there
Following us everywhere
Judging us, mocking us,
fooling us
Well its time we discuss
Why we chose to live
Your spotlight we do not
forgive
Bigger things is our plan
Saving a heart of
a simple man
We've been through hell
Now its time to get well

Micki Hogan
©2019

A Ruby bring forth creativity
Amethyst protects from
those who believe
Prism crystals help me see
The Tiger's Eye welcomes harmony
Black Tourmaline's protection
builds a boundary
Wearing Jade surrounds
with purity

These are the stones that call to me

Micki Hogan
©2019

A peace offering is what I see
But the truth of it cannot be
The twisted offering escapes
Hoping it is not to late

69

Micki Hogan
©2019

**Magical Moments
Do come true for each of you
Hearts never subdued**

Haiku Poem

70

Star child gazes upon the Sun
Wondering of things to come
Gathering round the horizon
Looking at auras through
crystal prism

Stories of peace most welcomed

71

Micki Hogan
©2019

Dance into Oblivion
Sing without hesitation
Paint a world you desire
Pen a tale filling hearts fire
Feel essence of music's beat
Poetic words make circle complete
Grab hold of life's calling
Careful now the worlds watching
Collide secret realms
Journey long fortelled

Micki Hogan
©2019

Awaken your 5 senses
While invoking 4 elements
A Prodigy sees 3 moments
An Unseen future of 2 planets
Until they become.. 1

73

Micki Hogan
©2019

Transcending beauty astounds
As heaven kisses the Earth
The angels trumpet sound
Grace extends with amazing girth
Humility knows no bounds
Compassion felt from birth
Love so very profound

74

The bells rang loudly in <u>Paris</u> today
<u>Notre Dame</u> fell to our dismay
A nation mourns as the <u>fires</u> blaze
All reaching out to blessed <u>sanctuary</u>

75

Thunderheads form in distance
Lush green grass
welcomes it
Red Robin's sing
a morning song
Young blossoms bloom
vibrant and strong
Colors of Spring burst alive
No longer in Winter do they hide

Micki Hogan
©2019

I don't think you understand
what I've been stressing
This message I've been getting
I watch the world sway
back and forth
A pendulum of connection,
once pointed true north
Now spins out of control
Time stops once more
Balance is the only way
To make it to another day

77

Mountains so pristine
Ice shimmers
Glistening
Just beyond the river Yellowstone
And where the Buffalo once roamed
The sunset sets in the Big Sky
Captivated by the passer by

Micki Hogan
©2019

Gently crimson clouds
Sun kissed with morning bliss
The Spring Equinox so profound
Winds of change bring warmth
To the ravaged Earth
Hear the Raven's sound
She calls across the land
Healing it with stature so grand

Micki Hogan
©2019

Power ascending within my head
This moment I no longer dread
Enter a shift in gravity
Just a quarter past eternity
Follow the signs
A part of the grand design
Hidden marking sees her through
While a muse pens her truth
A medium seeks the past
Will the future be told at long last

Micki Hogan
©2019

Dreams break free from the unseen
Embracing the things that be
Tread lightly where prisms fail
Says quietly the Nightingale
Gaze upon the Moonbeams dance
Catch the rays of Sunshine
at first glance
Lock them in your pocket
Keep them safe

Micki Hogan
©2019

Slow down the hourglass
Sands seep through by chance
Broken paths that time forgot
But not by the enlightened heart

Micki Hogan
©2019

I hear the call to one and all
Eye wide open
A blessing complete spiritual
A messenger to those who listen
Welcoming light as it glistens
mystic seer pens the truth
Daughter of revolution from birth
Adopted by an angel with white hair
Live long the grace of mother Earth
white knight prepares to stand tall
light called him from birth after all
To protect the human plight
He watches over
until the time comes
For he knows only love
can be the only path chosen
Two souls from worlds apart
Both guided by sacred light
Spared by those
who caused such a fright
We welcome the journey ahead
Both eyes fully awakened
With the silence of knowing heart

Micki Hogan
©2019

Tender is the somber song
A calling from within
Awakens after so long
Many do not know
the human plight
All one must do is
Embrace the Light

84

Micki Hogan
©2019

Those born with a veil
live life to the fullest
living on Earth in hindsight
Each moment
one invokes the power of the light
Embracing each moment
holding it tight
Even in the darkest of nights
Never let go...

85

No monuments needed,
no need to be seen,
we know you are there.
Always watching for those who care
secrets never to be told,
passed down from the time of old

Micki Hogan
©2019

The Lion sits quietly waiting
To hear the pyramids call
Waiting to pounce
Like a mighty king
He watches the snake coiled
Quietly eating on thyself
Golden king gazes upon obelisk
The tower topped in copper
Underneath the sun by day
the moon by night
Rhodium crossed keys unlock gates
The owl watches never hesitates
Feel the vibration from within
Hand signals welcome friends
A future leads to a sacred path
Etched in stone
Sheep cannot see the light
But the Loins guard
will protect them tonight

Micki Hogan
©2019

I feel within the grace from God
The giver of Light from above
I feel with each step Mother Earth
I feel pain we have caused her
Together they bring unity to us
Uniting creating life.
For them I trust.
I hear the future of technology
Calling me with such longing.

Micki Hogan
©2019

A journey told across the sands of time
Broken messages left
in ancient stone
Hymns speaking legends;
lyrical rhymes
Seven Pyramids
hide the catacombs
Hidden deep underneath
the golden shrines
Each continent holds a secret so old
Elder locks held safe by
the numbers prime
Passed down throne to throne,
secrets un-shown
Tempus moments aged
in sandstone and lime
Others deep in the forest over-grown
One frozen palace shimmers;
so divine
Patterns cross the globe secrets;
so unknown
The secrets hidden protect
the bloodlines
The path begins at
the unmarked tombstone

89

Micki Hogan
©2019

Behold Newton's Third Law
Silver penned Calligraphy
What was Seen
cannot be Unseen
One Thousand Stones
carefully placed in rows
Live by Sword,
die by Sword
Invoke Peace
if that is what you Seek
Look where Floating Spheres
glow at night
Always hidden in Hindsight

90

Infinite numbers circle
Round Prime Meridian
Follow the Roseline
To the 45th parallel
The truth of the Code
Past down from time old
The sacred language
We all speak
Art, poetry and science
Music and Dance
All to patterns that repeat
Chaos unfolds
As the code is retold

91

Micki Hogan
©2019

Bring to me the message
I long to hear
To where Elephant sleeps
Meditation and Observation
Journey through Canyons of Rocks
Statues on Copper domes point the way
Next to faces etched in stone
A warrior points alone
Follow his path
To where next I long to know

92

Micki Hogan
©2019

Visions of future come to pass
Technology in harmony
At long last
But in truth, face same fears
Without Mother Earth
End is near
Ashes to Ashes
Dust to Dust
Without Oil and Water
All joints will rust
Messengers of night listen well
For this truth to you I entrust

Micki Hogan
©2019

Deep within the forest green
Hidden underneath lush canopy
A forest nymph does her dance
Invoked moonlit sacred trance
In the dark eyes reflect
As animals watch in delight
She guards the forest lore

For she's old as the Sycamore

94

Micki Hogan
©2019

Listen to Mother Earth
Do not test her
Volcanic Eruptions
Asteroids sneak by
Panic unfolds
Water rises beyond thresholds
Fires burn
Through painted canyons
Panic in streets
Equal to every reaction
Mother Earth calls her name
Begging world please
Do not take me vain

95

Micki Hogan
©2019

Messages received
Patterns step forth
Welcome those who believe
Embrace the light
Even in the darkest of nights
The ballad has been sung
Harmonic patterns calling forth
To secrets long foretold
Graceful is the power within
Humility is where to begin

96

Micki Hogan
©2019

Embrace law of attraction
Do not make it a foe
For Newton Thirds Law
Speaks truth you know
Look beneath unknown soldier
For treasures long bestowed
Read between lines
White haired angels
Speak unseen words again
Descendants Three Five Five
Could be still alive

97

Micki Hogan
©2019

Captivating by rising moon
Welcoming nights mystic way
Fireflies dance in chaotic tune
Inception of thoughts sway
I welcome each lesson I am gifted
None knowing three unknown things
I will never say
Secret language of hands
What other secrets shall come my way

98

That's all there is
There is no more
Close the book, open it again
Read these poems once more
There are secrets within
Solve the puzzle within time
For these are the poetic musings

99

Micki Hogan
©2019

# of a rambling mind

Works by Micki Hogan

Chapter Books
Weeping Willow Book One: Rapture
Lost Behind the Looking Glass

Poetry Books
Seeking Revelations
Midnights Book of Lullabies
Fairy's Book of Lullabies I
Fairy's Book of Lullabies II
No Strings Attached

Kindle Quick Reads
Lady In White
Immortal Devotion
Eternally Intertwined
Before the Sentinals Came
Leaving Las Vegas
Primal Devotion

100

Micki Hogan
©2019

The Poetic Musings of a Rambling Mind

Her poem "Behind Glass Eyes"
won 2009 poem of the year
"Legacy Writers of Harmony Pub"

101

Micki Hogan
©2019